They
Aren't
Visitors

They are us

Patty sat on her porch watching out over the valleys down below her. She wasn't shocked at the scene playing out, she had always known that sooner or later the world would go to hell in a handbasket. Her thoughts lately had leaned toward civil uprising, things had seemed to be heading in that direction. This wasn't what she expected but it had been on the list of possibilities. She didn't know how things would play out but she had known the day would come and she liked having a front row seat for the show.

She and Kevin were as prepared as they could be for whatever was going to happen. Their lifestyle meant they could get through times when weather or circumstances kept them from being able to leave the mountain. They were mostly self sufficient, only going to town about once a month for staples at the market, anything they could order in bulk online would be waiting for them at the post office, and a stop at the feed store took care of the animals. They grew or made most of what they needed. They had been laughed at and made fun of but other people's approval wasn't their goal in life. Being left alone was their idea of success, being told how to live by the government (or anyone else) was not high on their list of priorities.

The government had been over-reaching more and more lately, people who had not been bothered by rules and regulations before were starting to understand those who were protesting, but they dealt with things differently. It seemed like every month a new group popped up with a grievance. Each demographic felt as though they had been singled out and targeted. The talking heads on the news seemed to take pleasure in stirring the pot and causing divisiveness, creating news instead of reporting it. Patty could see for herself the difference in what was portrayed on the news and what was really happening.

A train horn echoing up the mountain caught her attention, picking up her binoculars she focused on the tracks where they snaked along the bottom of the mountain on the far side of one of the valleys. There were three engines pulling boxcars that stretched for about half a mile, several tankers and a dozen flat cars with their loads covered by tarps, all being pushed by two more engines and heading south. The trains had been a clue that something was coming. Normally only two or three trains ran during the night and they mostly carried gravel, lumber and cars. Over the past few months there had been multiple trains running late every night, all carrying military equipment. There had been miles of tanks, armored vehicles, oversized crates were on flat cars, boxcars filled with the unknown and tankers filled with chemicals. Another clue had been the helicopters flying low in formation, sounding like drum beats bouncing off the mountains and the large military transport planes heading south in the morning and north in the evening.

There had been nothing about any of it on the news or in the papers. The internet was full of conspiracy theories. Some people had logical, well thought out arguments and were able back up their reasoning, others were so disorganized that you couldn't figure out what they thought. One thing had been certain, something was happening and it involved the armed forces.

This wasn't just the shuffling around of supplies and vehicles between bases, stuff was being moved all over the country. There had been photos of trains and convoys from every state. Little used bases in the middle of nowhere suddenly had the populations of small cities. Reserve units had been called up without being told where they were going. Overseas units had been brought back stateside but not sent home, they were being housed on bases. She and Kevin had heard the helicopters hovering in the valley around three in the morning and had gotten out of bed to see what was happening. Their home was tucked back up in a holler above a gap in the mountains. Sitting on their front porch there was a view of mountain tops going off into the distance, to the right of the gap there was a valley that ran southeast, to the left of the gap the valley went mostly north with a westward drift. Each valley had a small town and they were both dark, there were no lights in either valley and the mountains were dark. Up here they had solar and wind power but looking up from below you had to know where to look to see them. They had turned off all of the lights anyway, cell service and the internet were also gone. Kevin had brought the old AM/FM radio out onto the porch and they had been able to pick up some broadcast from amatuer operators. Things were the same all over, reports seemed consistent with what she was looking at. She and Kevin had been in Florida after the hurricanes and had been under martial law, that's what she was seeing now. Roadblocks on the highways and troops patrolling the towns, jeeps at intersections in the more rural areas. Martial law was used to keep the peace and prevent looting in times or unrest or disaster, cities were the most vulnerable because of the dense populations. Usually little towns and rural areas were left to local authorities with military backup if needed. From the reports they were hearing and what they were seeing the entire country was under military control.

The government apparently expected mass panic and the troops had been dispatched to maintain control. Patty was sure there would be chaos but didn't see the point of it, running crazy in the streets and looting was something she never understood.

There would be others like Kevin and her that just sat back and watched, waiting to see what the outcome would be. There didn't seem to be any imminent danger of any kind.

The radio broadcast reported power being restored, and not long after sunrise they heard the emergency alert tone coming from their cell phones. The same broadcast was repeating on all tv and radio stations.

The national alert stated that everything was under control, there was no danger, there was no need for concern. Citizens were asked to stay in their homes and there would be a live broadcast from the president at noon eastern time.

Patty had always believed in what they now call Cryptids, things that had been told about in stories going back eons, in oral histories and cave paintings but there was no proof they ever existed.

People thousands of years ago on opposite sides of the planet drew the same pictures and told the same stories. It always made her laugh when some long extinct species was suddenly found alive and well. Scientist were always having to correct themselves about things they told us were absolute. People dismiss the possibility of Bigfoot or dragons because they want modern proof, they ignore the ancient proof. Patty thought the ancient people knew a lot more than modern man gave them credit for. The same architecture had been used all over the planet, from the hinges to the pyramids, that wasn't coincidence. She believed things used to be very different than what was commonly thought.

As a little girl she had read all the books that were on the shelves at her school libraries and local public libraries about things people didn't believe in. Even when she was young it made sense to her that if every populated continent on the planet had cave painting and stories of aliens and hairy wildmen there must be something to it. It was logical to believe that in all the vast expanses of wild on this planet that there were undiscovered species and in all the vast expanse of space we couldn't be the only planet with life. All of the ancient peoples had tales of sky people, the Bible says there are other beings. Patty didn't understand people that were adamant that such things could not exist. Some people had their own perception of reality and couldn't be swayed without seeing for themselves.

The announcement from the president started half an hour late, he read a prepared statement as he sat behind his desk in his office. After he was done words scrolled up the screen repeating what he had said.

The gist of the situation was that extraterrestrials have been on this planet for millennia and were in contact with world leaders. It seemed our little planet was part of a galactic territorial dispute that was going on and benevolent aliens were going to protect us from the evil aliens that planned to invade and take over the globe. The citizens should remain calm and obey the local and military authorities who were there for safety and order. They were told that there would be sights in the sky that would be disturbing to some but there would be no danger. The government had everything under control.

Patty wasn't surprised at what she heard and wondered if she was to the age that nothing shocked her anymore or if the full impact of the news just hadn't sunk in yet. Either way she had no control over the situation so she decided to be an educated spectator and went to get her laptop and see if the internet was back up so she could do research. Having no luck getting online she started going through the radio dial listening to the antenna broadcast she could pick up. There were a few that seemed to have known for years about our planet being a strategic location in the galaxy. Our resources and habitability make us a very desirable piece of property for distant species that want to expand their territory. It seemed that our globe had been the property of a peaceful empire and had been under their protection since the beginning but a warlord has decided to take us to use as an outpost for further exploration beyond our solar system. The beings that had been living among us since before history saw us as students and helped us advance by educating us, the invaders saw us as pest to be eradicated. Peace talks and negotiations were going on between the species, there were war ships orbiting the planet.

Other broadcast reported panic, riots, looting and the other things the military was put in place to deal with. People who were unable to cope were committing suicide, others were wandering the streets in disbelief, churches were overflowing with people seeking answers. Hospitals and jails were filling quickly. In smaller rural communities people seem to being taking things pretty well and going about their daily lives for the most part. There were reports of people gathering outside of the

White House and the UN building. Later in the afternoon through repeated transmissions reports from other countries started coming in. First from Canada and Mexico, then from countries further south. Things seemed to be the same for them, areas with more dense populations were having more problems than the farmlands and low population areas. News from the islands filtered up through Florida and they didn't seem to be having any real problems other than those that couldn't believe what was happening and were not handling it well. There were remote places that only heard what was happening by radio or word of mouth.

As the sun set Kevin brought out the telescope and hooked it into the laptop so they could view it on the screen while they had supper.

News from Russia and Europe had been translated and was being passed on in English. In countries where there was already unrest and they didn't have the resources to control the population things got bad pretty fast. Cities were on fire and people were fleeing with no place to go. The Vatican and Mecca had people being crushed to death in the crowds coming to pray. Reports from Africa and Asia proved Patty's theory that people were the same all over the world. The higher the concentration of humans the more problems there were, panic and fear are contagious. People going out to loot and riot encouraged others to do the same, mob mentality. When the population is low and one or two people act out they are quickly dealt with. Some people still didn't believe what they were being told, proof would be necessary. On the laptop display there was a distant steak that crossed the screen unbelievably fast, widening the view revealed other steaks zipping past intermittently, they were too far away and moving too fast to focus on but there was definitely something going on out there. Scanning the rest of the sky showed a pinpoint light that was moving slower than the others and seemed to be getting closer. The light had grown to the size of and shape of a grain of rice when it became apparent that it had been several ships lined up one behind the other, still too far away to focus on. They split and fanned out in different directions , there were dozens of them that seemed to be forming some kind of grid or net. Patty and Kevin debated weather these ships were the offense or defense, and soon the same query was being played out on the radio. It may have been out of hope but popular opinion fell in favor of it being the aliens on our side building a safety perimeter to protect us. Some of the lights in the distant sky continued to grow as they came closer before dividing into multiple lights and forming another grid closer to Earth. They were close enough to see what they were. Multistoried tubular ships, they were moving too quickly still to get details. Radio accounts had some ships taking positions near enough to be seen without a telescope.

Through the night the light show continued, the number of spaceships that were out there was unbelievable. They were preparing for a major battle.

Around sunrise television services were given back to the channels to resume broadcasting their own programming. The news channels had their talking heads interviewing every alien expert they could get a camera on, military experts were giving their opinions while adamantly denying they had any knowledge of aliens. Pictures and videos of the UFOs started being shown. Worldwide there were scenes of chaos and prayer vigils, people coming together in different ways.

The president scheduled another announcement for noon and was almost an hour late giving the pundits more time to speculate on what he would have to say but none of them were close to guessing correctly. His message informed the people of the nation that our planet had been infiltrated by bad aliens that he referred to as Species R, these infiltrators had been here for hundreds if not thousands of years and had used their advantages to reach high levels of power and positions around the world. Our current president and some very trusted people around the world along with the good aliens, called Species P, had been working behind the scenes to quietly identify the infiltrators. Some of them had already been dealt with in various ways. Starting today squads would be sent out worldwide to round up some very powerful people, the president emphasized that these people were not Earthlings no matter how beloved some of them were. They were Species R and their objective was to kill off most of us, the ones that weren't killed would be enslaved. After the announcement the newsrooms went into overdrive speculating on the identities of the infiltrators. The president's supporters were confident that every word was true and they trusted him to do the right thing, those who opposed him were sure that it was all lies and he was taking advantage of the situation. By late afternoon there were videos coming in of military squads storming homes and offices of politicians, actors and millionaires. Planes were being stopped on runways as some tried to flee. Yachts were boarded at sea, and remote cabins were raided. There seemed to be nowhere they could hide, consensus was they had been tracked since they were identified as infiltrators. Around midnight the first video came in of a military transport plane landing in Cuba and the passengers being marched into the military prison there. All night, faces of the elite and celebrity aliens filled the news channels. Patty noticed they all had the same soulless look in their eyes.

Shock and disbelief at the whole situation seemed to rule the news networks, some were outraged and some were smug. Two anchors were handcuffed and led off of the set of a major outlet by one of the military squads. People started to become distrustful of those around them, accusations led to fights.

As the craziness went on in the rest of the world, Patty kept an eye on the laptop monitor. There had been a bright flash far out in space followed by several smaller flashes. The flashes spread, there seemed to be some type of firefight going on. Swarms of smaller fighter ships exited some of the larger tube ships. From the porch it looked like an extreme meteor shower with stars exploding.

The war went on overnight, getting closer and brighter. The scenes on the television looked like a science fiction movie as they showed video from high powered telescopes around the world.

After sunrise the news changed to the situation in the cities getting worse. Commercial trucking and trains weren't running, preventing groceries and supplies from getting to stores. The military was passing out food boxes, diapers and some other items but the people were unhappy. The stores had been looted and set on fire, the fires spread. People were killing each other in the streets. The troops were doing the best they could but they were under attack themselves in some places. Gangs would overrun the area and kill the soldiers taking their weapons and vehicles. The noon statement from the president assured citizen that more help was on the way and those troubled places would be dealt with swiftly. There would be a curfew in place and increased checkpoints to help calm tensions. Repeatedly it was stressed that everyone should remain calm and shelter in place, people were asked to go out only when needed. There were assurances that the battle in the sky was under control and the planet was safe.

As the days wore on Patty and Kevin went about life the same as before. The animals needed tending to and so did the garden. Repairs to the chicken coop were made and a fallen tree was chopped and ready to use for firewood when the weather cooled.

News on the radio and TV reported the invaders had been defeated, the cities had been restored to order for the most part. Supplies were getting to the markets on a limited basis. Martial law was still in place nationwide.

A week after it all began, their friend Jim rode over on horseback. He brought news of others that lived up in the mountains and word of what was happening in the valleys.

For those that lived like they did there had been little effect. The little towns below had adapted quickly. Farmers markets were busy, filled with people that usually shopped at the chain grocery stores. Butchers, dairies and local shops selling homemade goods, were hiring help to handle the increase in business. The mill had gone from being mostly tourist attraction to having people waiting in line.

Bartering had always been a way of doing business for people in the mountains and was now being used in the towns as a way to get goods and services needed. Neighbors were helping each other as they adjusted to the changes.

Over time more news came out uncovering how deeply the aliens on both sides had infiltrated the highest levels of government and society worldwide. Going back generations Species R had been acquiring wealth and buying their way into powerful positions. They ran media outlets, movie companies and major corporations. Species R had been influencing the people of earth through these businesses. They used movies, music, news, toys, marketing and anything else available to divide people and make the unacceptable seem mainstream, eroding morals and religion. The masses had been told how and what to think by the aliens that wanted to destroy them. Their goal had been to weaken us in preparation for the invasion. Their positions in government had been used to pass laws limiting citizen freedoms, they had filled books with rules and regulations telling everyone it was for their own good. Little by little they had taken the freedom from what had been a free country. They had convinced people the government knew what was best for them and the people had willing handed over their rights one by one. Taxes were raised taking money to pay for all of the free things promised in return. The last election was supposed to have been the final takeover. Species R had the presidential front runner of one party. The win was assured. Once in office their puppet would fill the cabinet with aliens, they already had their picks lined up for appointed positions. They would have control and would get rid of anyone that opposed them. Species R had been here for hundreds of years and this was to be the prize they had been after, control of the president meant control of the military. A global war would greatly reduce the number of humans and those that survived would be used as slave labor to supply and serve the outpost that would be established. Species P had been here since our beginning, they had nurtured and guided us. They wanted all planets to do well and work together. They were educators and guardians. They stepped in to protect their children from the bad guys. They had been watching and preparing, quietly putting their own operatives in place. They had been playing an elaborate game of chess without the opponent knowing they were part of the game. All of the pieces were put into place during the last campaign. Species R, along with many citizens were shocked when they lost the election to someone that wasn't even a politician.

Species R had started to panic and had been trying every tactic they could think of to discredit and disrupt the current administration because they knew their downfall was imminent. Those in the capitol building that were colluding with the bad guys started calling for impeachment. People had been hired to protest and riot in an effort to cause divisiveness, pitting demographics against each other. Mass shootings and school shooting caused finger pointing and fear mongering.

There had been some people that had started to wake up and see what was being done, they were speaking out trying to spread the word. Those people had been labeled conspiracy theorist and mocked. Internet groups and pages popped up in support of the new administration, these people were labeled as any derogatory term the opposition could come up with.

While all of this was playing out, Species P and the good guys had been working behind the scenes to end the plans of Species R and stop the invasion. Stacks of arrest warrants had been drawn up for aliens and those that had been knowingly helping them. Those that had been picked up during the mass arrest had been separated into two groups. One group consisted of Species R aliens, the other group was listed as traitors.

Punishment was swift for those in the Species R group, they had been flown to Cuba and within a month their deaths began. They had been unmasked one by one on live TV, proving they were alien and marched to a row of thirteen gallows. Politicians, millionaires and movie stars hanged for the world to see. The hangings went on from sunrise until sunset, with more planes landing each day full of those condemned to die.

The little used military bases that had been suddenly staffed were now prison encampments for the traitors. People who had used their power and position to aid the enemy thinking the enemy would reward them, in truth they would have been killed along with everyone else. They were declared enemies of the state, working for an enemy power and military tribunals were held. Some weak arguments were made on grounds of constitutionality but the country as a whole seemed to be accepting of the process. The first week prosecutors exhibited overwhelming evidence against groups of co-defendants. The first trial was against a group of twenty three formally high ranking government officials. Bank records, electronic communications, video surveillance, satellite tracking and damning documents were listed as evidence and after the detailed list was read aloud the first morning it was clear they were guilty. The defendants asked for plea agreements and were denied, they begged for mercy in open court. There were senators, judges and former cabinet members on their knees crying as they were sentenced to hang. Each day a new group made their appearance, the military worked with precision and expediency. The morning opened with the names of the defendants and the charges against them followed by the list of evidence compiled. The list would be exact and detailed so there was no defense, there were no plea deals and no mercy was given. At the end of the day each group, having been found guilty and sentenced to hang, would be added to those waiting to be loaded on a plane headed to Cuba.

The same scenario was being played out all over the planet. Different governments dealt with things in their own way but the results were the same. Cable news aired firing squads, beheadings and hangings around the clock. The world watched as they got used to their "new normal". People who had been paid trouble makers came to realize they had been paid by the bad guys, others realized they had been lied to their whole life by those they had elected to represent them, some sat back saying they had tried to warn us. Groups popped up defending Species R, they wanted proof they were bad guys and theorized Species P were actually using us to get rid of their enemies. Some of those people just couldn't accept the deception they had been living under, others thrived on controversy and took any opportunity to stir things up.

Things calmed as the days passed, the immediate trials and executions were carried out and transitioned into defendants that wanted to try putting on a defense in hopes of avoiding the gallows.

It became clear that some supplies and goods would no longer be on the market, entire corporations were brought down when their CEOs and boards were put to death. Some companies had been in business for the sole purpose of bringing down the country through their products. They had been intentionally poisoning both the bodies and minds of the population, weakening the country. Helping the enemy prepare us for takeover. Many Hollywood studios were out of business, owners, producers, directors, writers and stars all proven to have intentionally worked with the enemy to produce films and tv shows that were meant to degrade the morals and values of the population as a whole, normalizing what had been previously unthinkable. Indoctrinating people to accept government control and nanny states for their own good. Controlling what people see as acceptable and telling them what they should be outraged about. Violence had been inserted into every aspect of the entertainment industry, making rape and murder seem to be everyday occurrences that should be accepted. Music videos and online games depicted sex and violence going hand in hand. They used the guise of comedy to openly mock religion and those who believed in a higher power.

Owners of media outlets were proven to have used their newspapers, television news and internet pages to influence what people believed. Anchors admitted they blatantly lied on the air to their viewers in order to advance their agenda. Pictures and videos were used out of context with the intent of causing unrest and discord. They pointed fingers and placed blame where it didn't belong all while hiding the fact they were the bad guys.

Heads of colleges and universities admitted their agenda of indoctrination and misinformation. Teaching entire generations to do as they were told and not question authority. Their classes stressed the importance of trusting in the government to take care of them, they pushed an entitlement mindset to students brainwashing them into believing they should get everything they want just because they want it. These institutions handed out diplomas year after year to people that were deeply in debt to the government for student loans and unqualified to get employment that covered the payments much less living expenses. Many of these former students end up back at their parents and earning money by protesting.

Heads of religion confessed their evil deeds. Some tried using a "Devil made me do it" defense. Their fate was the same as those convicted before them.

All of the humans hanged had willing and voluntarily aided the enemy for personal gain. They had sold the fate of the human race for greed, or so they had thought. Very few showed any sympathy for those who had betrayed our planet.

Patty sat on the porch looking out at the night sky, now back to just the normal heavenly objects. The warships had gone to wherever it is warships go after a battle, the Species P patrol ships were still out there but far out of site.

Thinking about the changes that had happened over the last few months, Patty came to the conclusion that the overall outcome was positive.

Things were much more peaceful now, those that threatened the peace and continued wars were all gone. All of the soldiers were home with their families. During the looting and riots gang members, and bad guys in general, were dealt with by the military and would no longer be making trouble. Crime rates had dropped drastically. Martial law had come to an end. Local economies were booming. Corporations that had been responsible for factory farming were gone. The farmers had gone back to selling locally. People who made things suddenly had a market for their products. Everything from soap to jelly, pickles, and clothes had to come from somewhere and now people were getting it from their neighbors rather than some faceless company that had been selling them poison for years.

People were paying attention to what their kids were being taught and doing their own research into the subjects. They questioned what they were being told on the news and on the internet. People had finally awakened to the reality of the world around them and how it impacts them.

Housing prices were down nationwide, Beverly Hills and the area around D.C. had mansions listed for sale at rock bottom prices because most of them were now vacant.

From what was on television and the reports on the radio, things seemed to be generally the same worldwide. Peace, love and happiness. What more could anyone ask for?

Patty sat back in her rocking chair and smiled, wondering what would happen next.

THE
END

Made in the USA
Middletown, DE
23 November 2018